Featured at New Visions / New Voices
Festival at The Kennedy Center

Ramon Esquivel

Nocturnal

Wildboy Concepts
Seattle

NOCTURNAL

by

Ramon Esquivel

A Wildboy Concepts Book | Seattle 2013
www. Wildboyconcepts.com

Ramon Esquivel

Nocturnal

 Wildboy Concepts
Seattle

Fiction/ Drama

Nocturnal

Even good kids can do bad things. When four friends venture into the night to pull a prank, they end up engaging in a battle of wills. Three high school freshmen, Cisco, Ryker, and Rolly, try to sabotage the Senior Prank, but they are sabotaged themselves by Amelia. The friends choose sides and face off in a game of Dare. As it escalates to dangerous levels, will anyone have the courage to back down?

Author photo Darrah Parker Photography

Ramon Esquivel is a writer and teacher based in Seattle. His work has been seen in New York, Chicago and Washington D.C. He is the winner of the Bonderman Playwriting for Youth Workshop at Indiana Repertory Theater and the New Visions/New Voices at the Kennedy Center for the Performing Arts.

Cover photograph by Ashley Bell; design by Agnew Kyle

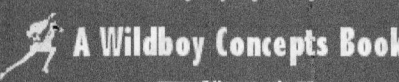

A Wildboy Concepts Book

www.wildboyconcepts.com

Notice

PRODUCTION NOTES

Nocturnal was developed at the 2008 New Visions / New Voices residency at John F. Kennedy Center for the Performing Arts in Washington, District of Columbia. The play premiered at Bloomington Playwrights Project in Bloomington, Indiana in January 2009.

CHARACTERS

CISCO. - a smart boy, 15

RYKER. - a small boy, 15

ROLLY. - a big boy, 16

AMELIA. - a tom boy, 16

SETTING

Night. The present. A suburb.

Running time: 40-50 minutes.

When produced with its companion piece Nasty, Nocturnal should play second.

The script calls for four settings: High School, Playground, Exterior of AMELIA.'s House, and a Train Trestle. In the BPP production, this was achieved through manipulation of a flexible set piece resembling playground jungle gym.

Nocturnal

(Darkness. Silence. Then a flashlight)

RYKER. *(offstage, through walkie-talkie)* Sector 1 clear. Sector 2?

(A second flashlight)

CISCO. (offstage, through a walkie-talkie)Sector 2 clear. Sector 3?

(silence)

Sector 3!

(A third flashlight)

ROLLY. *(offstage, not through a walkie-talkie)* Sector 3 clear!

RYKER. All units, go.

> (CISCO *and* RYKER *enter dressed as would-be saboteurs.*
>
> *Down a man, Ryker calls out*)

All units, go!

> (ROLLY *enters with a combat roll, similarly dressed and carrying a bag*)

CISCO. Those judo lessons are paying off, man.

ROLLY. Next time I get a walkie-talkie.

RYKER. Next time. Definitely.

ROLLY. I brought 'em.

CISCO. We promise.

RYKER. Keep an eye out.

> (*The boys stand outside the* HIGH SCHOOL. *They shine lights on a window with* "SENIORS!" *painted on it in fat bubble letters*)

CISCO. This it?

RYKER. Apparently.

ROLLY. This is the Senior Prank?

RYKER. Lame, uh? School-sanctioned vandalism. Vice Principal even supervised it.

CISCO. This paint comes right off.

ROLLY. Bubble letters. Their prank sucks.

RYKER. Let's improve it.

> (*Cisco and Ryker position flashlights to illuminate work area. Rolly pulls cans of spray-paint from bag and distributes them*)

ROLLY. Wait, how do you spell "sophomores" again?

CISCO. S-O-P-H-O-M-O-R-E-S.

ROLLY. Two o's?

CISCO. Three.

RYKER. Can't count either?

ROLLY. I meant three.

RYKER. Rolly, you do the S-O-P.

ROLLY. 'Kay.

RYKER. Cisco does H-O-M-O.

CISCO. Saw that coming.

RYKER. I got R-E-S and the exclamation point.

(*They paint and converse*)

CISCO. This paint washable?

ROLLY. Nope. Janitor will be scraping it off for days.

CISCO. Poor guy.

RYKER. He has to clean up Senior Prank crap anyway.

CISCO. Humiliating. There's no justice at this school.

ROLLY. Just figure that out?

RYKER. If you feel bad, clean it up.

CISCO. I'd earn service points for Honor Society.

ROLLY. Glad I'm not in Honor Society.

CISCO. Keep reaching for those stars, man.

RYKER. Cleaning it would be a good cover. But they'll make the sophomores do it.

CISCO. I used to think it was "soft-mores."

ROLLY. See? That's why I asked.

CISCO. Turns out it's derived from the Greek *sophisma*. To acquire wisdom or skill.

RYKER. Ah. *Sophisma*. Related to sophist? Purveyor of shallow knowledge?

CISCO. According to Plato.

ROLLY. You do this on purpose.

RYKER. *Sophisma*, not to be confused with Sappho, Classic poetess of the Island of Lesbos.

CISCO. The Island of Lesbos must have been so hot.

RYKER. I doubt Sappho was hot.

CISCO. She was Classic hot. Big ol' boobies.

ROLLY. Awesome.

CISCO. Big ol' booty.

ROLLY. Me likey!

CISCO. I gotta get myself a big poster of Sappho.

ROLLY. Was there really an island of lesbians?

RYKER. Welcome to the world of Classics.

ROLLY. Man, I should've taken Latin with you guys, instead of Spanish.

CISCO. *Pero Espanol es una lengua muy interesante tambien.*

ROLLY. Is that Spanish?

CISCO. Just worry about English.

RYKER. Let's have a look.

(*They pick up flashlights and step back to admire their work. Their crude "SOPHOMORES" covers the bubbly "SENIORS" beneath it*)

CISCO. Beauty, eh?

(*Improvised compliments on each other's artwork*)

RYKER. Sweet revenge.

ROLLY. Yeah, Ryker. This ought to teach those seniors not to shove your head down a toilet.

RYKER. What did I tell you about that?

(Cisco and Rolly laugh. Ryker punches Rolly)

ROLLY. "Don't bring up the swirly."

RYKER. I meant it.

CISCO. We're sorry, man.

RYKER. I still haven't forgiven you guys for ditching me that day.

CISCO. We're here now, aren't we?

ROLLY. Risking our lives ...

CISCO. —And academic reputations ...

ROLLY. —Uh, yeah. But why are we giving sophomores the credit?

RYKER. Really? Three explanations weren't enough?

ROLLY. I mean, I get it, but ...

CISCO. —You want us to paint "FRESHMEN?"

ROLLY. We are freshmen. We deserve the glory.

RYKER. No capacity for strategic thinking.

CISCO. Seniors know that juniors aren't stupid enough to do this. And they know freshmen aren't brave enough.

RYKER. Even if we are.

ROLLY. And sophomores?

RYKER. Sophomores are stupid enough and brave enough.

CISCO. And will therefore feel the senior wrath.

ROLLY. That's really smart.

RYKER. This is the stuff we learn in Latin class.

(*A sharp pea whistle from off-stage*)

ROLLY. Run!

RYKER. Lights!

(*Flashlights off*)

CISCO. Rendezvous!

(*In darkness, Cisco, Ryker and Rolly flee. Rolly runs into a garbage can*)

ROLLY. Man down!

RYKER. (*off-stage*) Damn it, Rolly!

ROLLY. Don't say my name, Ryker!

(*Another pea whistle, closer.*
Silence. Darkness.
A flashlight scans the crime scene. A garbage can is over-turned. A window has been
vandalized. Twice. A figure enters, picks up a can of spray paint, and then exits)

(THE PLAYGROUND, *a few blocks away. A big playground structure*

dominates the space.

RYKER *enters first, shaken. He does not notice when* CISCO *enters*)

CISCO. Hey.

(RYKER *startles*)

RYKER. Someone screwed us.

CISCO. We don't know that. Security guard just did his job.

RYKER. We did two nights of recon! The security guard checks outside the

school at midnight, two o'clock and four o'clock. It's 2:27 now.

CISCO. Yeah, but he could've changed his ...

RYKER. —Two nights! We watched him go back in at 2:13. His next round

isn't due for another hour and a half.

CISCO. A neighbor probably saw us. Or heard us. We're not ninjas.

RYKER. Someone screwed us.

(ROLLY *enters*)

CISCO. Here comes Train Wreck.

RYKER. Limping like an old man.

ROLLY. You guys are dicks.

CISCO. You really nailed that garbage can.

ROLLY. It was dark. And thanks for ditching me.

RYKER. Sucks to be ditched by your friends, yeah?

ROLLY. Banged up my knee. It better not mess up my judo.

CISCO. I wouldn't worry about that.

RYKER. Someone screwed us.

ROLLY. Yeah?

RYKER. Definitely.

CISCO. Maybe.

RYKER. Only we three knew about this.

ROLLY. I didn't say anything.

RYKER. No one at school?

ROLLY. Who would I tell?

RYKER. True, we are your only friends. Did you?

CISCO. Me? What about you?

RYKER. Why would I blow my own plan?

CISCO. Blackmail.

ROLLY. Blackmail!

RYKER. What? If I was gonna blackmail you, I would ...

(*A pea whistle from nearby*)

ROLLY. He followed us!

CISCO. Run!

(*All three scatter and exit.*

    AMELIA *enters carrying a can of spray paint and wearing a whistle*

around her neck. She calls after the guys)

AMELIA. You left some evidence behind!

CISCO. (*offstage*) Amelia!

    (*Amelia blows the whistle again, sets down the paint, and exits.*

The BOYS enter and examine the can)

RYKER. Damn it, Cisco!

ROLLY. She blew the whistle?

CISCO. Who dropped a can?

RYKER. Stupid Roland.

ROLLY. Don't call me that.

RYKER. (*calling off*) You're gonna pay for this, Amelia!

    (*Cisco starts laughing*)

ROLLY. What's so funny?

CISCO. Come on, she burned us good.

RYKER. What if we got caught?

CISCO. We didn't.

RYKER. But what if we did? Security guard could have heard her whistle and nabbed us.

CISCO. But he didn't.

RYKER. "Zero Tolerance," remember? Getting expelled doesn't look so hot on a transcript. No Notre Dame for you, Cisco.

CISCO. Relax. We're safe.

ROLLY. We told you specifically: "Don't say anything to Amelia.."

CISCO. I know. But you know how things kind of slip out sometimes?

RYKER. Never. I always say exactly what I mean to say.

CISCO. You don't ever talk to girls. You don't know how it is.

RYKER. Why did she screw up my plan?

CISCO. She hates the people in her class. When I told her about our plan, she wanted to go. I said no.

ROLLY. Ryker would have shat his pants if Amelia showed up.

CISCO. I know, right? She was still pissed.

RYKER. I told you to never trust that little ...

CISCO. —Don't.

ROLLY. Whoa. Defending her honor.

RYKER. Oh, he's always so chivalrous when it comes to Amelia. I have no idea what you see in her.

CISCO. You asked her out last year.

ROLLY. Eighth grade boat dance.

RYKER. I was desperate.

CISCO. Especially when she turned you down.

RYKER. Whatever. That was middle school. We're in high school now. We got real women now.

ROLLY. Passing on the left, on the right ...

CISCO. —Never stopping ...

RYKER. —My point is: Those women are hot and Amelia's not.

ROLLY. Yeah, Amelia's like ... she's like a guy.

CISCO. You guys are just pissed because she burned us. Give her some credit for that.

RYKER. She can do no wrong. All because she gave you a little ...

CISCO. —Don't say it.

ROLLY. Wait, what?

(Ryker laughs)

CISCO. I swear to God, Ryker ...

ROLLY. —Come on! What?

RYKER. Tell him. It's good ol' Rolly.

ROLLY. You hooked up with her!

CISCO. No!

RYKER. Not quite.

CISCO. We just kind of kissed and stuff.

RYKER. "And stuff." What's this, "And stuff?"

ROLLY. You? When?

CISCO. This summer.

RYKER. His lifelong dream. Didn't quite work out though, did it?

CISCO. Drop it.

ROLLY. Details.

CISCO. I'm not giving details.

ROLLY. Like hell you're not. I want details. I need details.

RYKER. Throw him some scraps.

CISCO. I told her I wouldn't say anything.

ROLLY. You told Ryker!

CISCO. He used witchcraft on me.

RYKER. Oh, my wicked, wicked ways. But the details are boring. It was —
how should I say it? — an aborted attempt by Cisco.

ROLLY. You got her pregnant?

CISCO. No! God!

RYKER. Nice one.

CISCO. See why I didn't tell you? You're so stupid about sex.

ROLLY. Don't say I'm stupid.

RYKER. Just tell him.

CISCO. I shouldn't have even told you.

RYKER. Don't wanna break her trust? She broke yours.

CISCO. She burned us. Get over it.

RYKER. She crossed me. That calls for revenge.

ROLLY. Yes. Revenge! (*to Cisco*) You're gonna give me details later.

CISCO. You going after her?

RYKER. Yup.

CISCO. Now?

RYKER. Massive retaliation.

ROLLY. "Revenge is a dish that is best served cold."

RYKER. Well said, *Wrath of Khan*.

CISCO. Look, if we wake up her family, they'll kill us.

ROLLY. They'll kill you.

RYKER. Like you said, she burned us. If she's really as "cool, not hot" as you say, she'll take some heat in return.

ROLLY. What did you have in mind?

(*Ryker pulls out his can of spray-paint*)

RYKER. One word, four letters, written on her window.

ROLLY. What?

RYKER. S-L-U-T.

CISCO. No way.

ROLLY. "Slut."

RYKER. Very good.

CISCO. She'll know you did it.

RYKER. Of course she will. And when she comes after me, I'll tell her what you told me.

CISCO. No, you won't.

RYKER. Watch me.

ROLLY. I hear she really got around last year.

(*Cisco punches Rolly in the arm*)

CISCO. She didn't.

ROLLY. I just hear rumors, you know?

CISCO. Those rumors piss her off ...

RYKER. —Well, she pisses me off. Hand over your walkie-talkie.
(*Cisco gives his walkie-talkie to Rolly*) Get your can, Rolly.

(Cisco picks up the can on the ground)

CISCO. Don't do this, guys.

ROLLY. Give me the cans.

CISCO. Our moms are friends. She tells her mom everything, who tells my mom everything ...

RYKER. —Don't be such a gay boy.

CISCO. Come on! Sex and a Catholic mom? She will cry first, and then she will slap the hell out of me when she finds out my friends wrote "SLUT" on Amelia's window.

ROLLY. Your mom wouldn't hit you.

CISCO. She would if you wrote "SLUT." Then my dad will take his turn.

ROLLY. Yeah, your dad might hit you.

RYKER. *(to Cisco)* You done?

CISCO. Next, they'll carry my body over to Amelia's, where her mom will cry, slap me, and then let her dad and brothers pound me some more.

ROLLY. Amelia would beat you down too.

CISCO. You know she would. And ... yeah. And Amelia will hate me. Guess that won't matter because I'll be dead. Thanks to you guys.

(*Beat*)

RYKER. Look. I'm not evil. I'll compromise. Instead of painting "SLUT" on her window, we'll put "HARLOT."

CISCO. Jeez, Ryker.

RYKER. Nobody knows what "harlot" means anymore.

ROLLY. What does it mean?

CISCO. "Slut."

RYKER. It's the best offer you're gonna get. A girl burned me. I must restore balance to the universe. Give Rolly. your paint.

(*Rolly extends his hand to take the can, but Cisco sprays him*)

ROLLY. Ow!

CISCO. "Ow," he says. It's paint. And it's going ...

(*Cisco points the can at the ground and continually sprays it*)

RYKER. —Just take it!

(*Cisco evades Rolly, all the while spraying and wasting the paint*)

CISCO. Going ...

RYKER. —Never mind, we don't need it.

(*Cisco moves before Ryker can react*)

I got mine.

(*Cisco tackles Ryker and takes his can. Ryker gets a few punches in before Cisco is up and running again holding both cans and wasting their paint. Rolly joins in the pursuit but Cisco uses the playground equipment to his advantage. The boys improvise insults and taunts. The chase continues until the paint is exhausted*)

CISCO. Gone. Oh.

ROLLY. (*winded*) Thank God.

RYKER. Where did this spine come from?

CISCO. It's strategy.

RYKER. Strategy?

CISCO. Look at yourselves. Red paint all over. The same red paint used to ruin the Senior Prank. Uh-oh.

RYKER. Damn it.

ROLLY. We're dead.

CISCO. Better get it off before it sets. Remember, it's not washable.

RYKER. You screwed us more than Amelia did. But she still has to pay. Rolly, we need more paint.

ROLLY. We don't have any more.

RYKER. Your dad paints houses for a living. You got paint. And we're back to writing "slut."

CISCO. I won't let you.

RYKER. How are you gonna stop us?

CISCO. I'll think of something.

RYKER. We met in sixth grade Chess Club. In all the matches we've played, how many times have you beaten me? Zero.

CISCO. This isn't chess.

RYKER. Everything is chess. And your queen is a goner. Let's go, Roland.

(*Ryker exits*)

ROLLY. Don't call me that!
    (*to Cisco*) Come on, we'll talk him out of it.

CISCO. Now you're on my side?

ROLLY. This will be fun. And Amelia deserves some payback.

CISCO. Just come over to my house. We'll play The Box or something.

ROLLY. I've beaten all your games already.

CISCO. Show me how to beat the Necromancer in *Elder World III*.

ROLLY. You still can't beat the Necromancer? He's doesn't even have death runes. You even know where the elven bolo is?

CISCO. The cave?

ROLLY. The grotto! How can you not ... ?

RYKER. (*offstage*) —Rolly!

ROLLY. Come over tomorrow and help me beat *Joyride Miami*. I got the code f or unlimited armor-piercing bullets.

CISCO. I'm gonna stop you guys.

ROLLY. Don't worry. I won't let it get out of hand.

    (*Rolly exits. Cisco drops empty cans in the trash and exits*)

(AMELIA'S HOUSE, *exterior.*

CISCO *enters. Light in Amelia's window on second floor is on*)

CISCO. Amelia.

(*throws pebbles at Amelia's window*)

Amelia!

(AMELIA *looks out*)

AMELIA. Burn, baby, burn!

CISCO. The hell were you thinking?

AMELIA. That it would be hilarious to scare you guys.

CISCO. Get down here, we need to talk.

AMELIA. Why?

CISCO. Ryker's on the warpath.

AMELIA. I can take him.

CISCO. Get down here anyway.

AMELIA. Hang on.

(*Amelia climbs down from window. She is wearing a soccer jersey and shorts*)

CISCO. You sleep in that?

AMELIA. It's my skin, yeah. Your paint job at the school sucks, by the way.

CISCO. Ryker's pissed at you.

AMELIA. Are you?

CISCO. Yeah.

AMELIA. Why?

CISCO. Because I trusted you.

AMELIA. I didn't touch your little prank. It's still there, lame as it is.

CISCO. Still ...

AMELIA. —Geek boys thinking you're all badass, sneaking out at night and painting a window.

CISCO. It's pretty badass taking on seniors.

AMELIA. But you guys running scared like that? And Rolly crashing into the garbage can?

CISCO. That was funny.

AMELIA. You gotta take some yourselves.

CISCO. You didn't mess up our artwork?

AMELIA. Didn't touch it. Nellie Reyes and Lilly Park are gonna freak when they see what you did to their window.

CISCO. Promise you won't give us away?

AMELIA. How long have you known me?

CISCO. My whole life.

AMELIA. And have I ever let you get hurt?

CISCO. You used to sit on my head when we were kids.

AMELIA. Okay, but recently?

CISCO. Guess not.

AMELIA. I even saved you from a few ass-kickings in middle school. You and your obnoxious friends.

CISCO. I know.

(*Beat*)

AMELIA. Forgive me?

CISCO. I guess.

AMELIA. Good.

CISCO. But those guys are still coming for you.

AMELIA. I can handle them. What are they gonna do?

CISCO. Spray paint your window.

AMELIA. And write what?

CISCO. Doesn't matter.

AMELIA. Cisco.

CISCO. Umm. "SLUT."

AMELIA. "SLUT?"

CISCO. They don't mean anything by it.

AMELIA. You tell them anything?

CISCO. No.

AMELIA. Swear?

CISCO. "Slut" doesn't mean anything.

AMELIA. Not to guys, maybe.

CISCO. I mean, Ryker calls me "gay" all the time, but who cares?

AMELIA. Answer my question: you tell them anything? And don't lie because I'll know it.

CISCO. ...

AMELIA. Of course you did.

CISCO. I'm sorry.

AMELIA. Even the nice guys are liars.

CISCO. I didn't give details.

AMELIA. "Details." Gross. What did you say?

CISCO. Just that, you know, you took pity on me and we fooled around a little. Kissing and stuff.

AMELIA. That's it?

CISCO. That's it.

AMELIA. That's not so bad. Had far worse said about me last year.

CISCO. I know.

AMELIA. But this year is gonna be different.

CISCO. It will.

AMELIA. That's really all you told those guys?

CISCO. Don't worry.

AMELIA. Because that Ryker always gives me these sleazy little grins when I pass him in the hall.

CISCO. He's just messing with you.

AMELIA. And Rolly? I don't want to know what goes through that kid's mind.

CISCO. No, you don't.

AMELIA. They on their way now?

CISCO. That's why I'm here.

AMELIA. You're backing me over your friends?

CISCO. Of course. You and I have been friends longer anyways.

AMELIA. Good to know where your loyalties lie.

CISCO. And I didn't want to get thrashed by your dad and brothers.

AMELIA. They wouldn't thrash you. They love you.

CISCO. I'm not taking any chances.

AMELIA. How much time do we have?

CISCO. They're washing off and getting more paint.

AMELIA. Gonna get my dad's gun.

CISCO. What?!

AMELIA. Joking. Go get the hose out.

(Amelia climbs up to her window and turns the light out. She climbs back down as Cisco pulls out a garden hose)

CISCO. Won't this wake up your family?

AMELIA. If we blew up dynamite, they would sleep right through it.

(*She gives Cisco the end of garden hose and turns on an external faucet*)

Put your thumb over the nozzle. See how far it shoots.

(*Cisco does this. They watch the spray*)

CISCO. It's freezing. Give it more.

(*Amelia turns up the pressure and then joins Cisco spraying the area*)

That's good range.

AMELIA. Easy with that. We don't want them to see us.

CISCO. Now what?

AMELIA. Behind the tree.

(*They hide*)

CISCO. Now what?

AMELIA. We wait.

(*They wait*)

CISCO. They might use toilet paper too. Rolly's big on TP-ing.

AMELIA. I bet his family goes through a lot of toilet paper.

CISCO. You just painted a picture in my mind of Rolly.'s mom sitting on the toilet. Thanks.

AMELIA. You're welcome.

(*They wait*)

CISCO. How's soccer?

AMELIA. Getting moved to midfield. Coach likes me because I'm aggressive.

CISCO. You're scary out there.

AMELIA. She says I'd be good in a bar fight.

CISCO. Don't coaches get fired for saying stuff like that?

AMELIA. She didn't take me to a bar.

CISCO. Your coach is hot.

AMELIA. She is.

CISCO. You got the hots for her too?

AMELIA. Everyone does.

CISCO. Think she'd go for me?

AMELIA. You're fifteen.

CISCO. I like older women. You know that.

AMELIA. Ugh. I'll tell her you're available.

CISCO. You just painted a picture in my mind of your coach ...

AMELIA. —Don't.

CISCO. Okay. But thanks.

AMELIA. You're welcome.

(*They wait*)

CISCO. This is wasting water, letting the hose run.

AMELIA. War is bad for the environment.

CISCO. We douse those guys with water, it will be war.

AMELIA. We can take them.

CISCO. I guess a little blood-letting between friends is healthy.

AMELIA. If they piss you off, so what? You move on. Get new friends.
That's how it works.

CISCO. We have a good time usually.

AMELIA. Hey. I know you're really here because you care about me.
And that's sweet of you.

CISCO. Let's stop talking like this. Please?

AMELIA. Okay. But thanks.

CISCO. You're welcome.

ROLLY. (*offstage*) Come on, it will be awesome!

RYKER. (*offstage*) No.

CISCO. Here they come.

AMELIA. Give me the hose.

> (*Amelia and Cisco duck down as* RYKER *and* ROLLY *enter.*
> *Ryker holds cans of spray paint. Rolly balances six rolls of toilet paper*)

ROLLY. It's kind of like My Thing.

RYKER. You don't even do it right.

ROLLY. I've done it a million times.

RYKER. Fine, just stop whining. Window first, though.

ROLLY. Which one is hers?

RYKER. That one.

ROLLY. Lights out. Think Cisco's up there? "Doing stuff?"

RYKER. They are not "doing stuff." Trust me.

(*Amelia glares at Cisco and gives him a shot from the hose. He silently screams*)

ROLLY. Should we do it?

RYKER. Yup.

ROLLY. I'm on it.

(*Rolly throws a roll of toilet paper. It bumps against the house, unfurled*)

RYKER. Rolly, what the hell?

ROLLY. Oops.

RYKER. What did I say? Window first, then your stupid toilet paper.

ROLLY. Sorry, I just get so excited.

RYKER. And you don't just throw the rolls at the house, stupid ...

ROLLY. —Don't call me ...

RYKER. —You unfurl them first.

ROLLY. How are you gonna get up to her window?

RYKER. Drop the TP and put me on your shoulders.

(*Rolly drops his rolls of toilet paper. Ryker gets on Rolly's shoulders while holding the paint cans. As he positions himself to write on the window …*)

AMELIA. Now!

(*Amelia douses Ryker and Rolly with water. They collapse on the ground and scream but they can only cower there and take it. Cisco unfurls the toilet paper and throws it at Ryker and Rolly*)

CISCO. Yield!

ROLLY. No!

RYKER. Let me go, Rolly!

(*More dousing, until …*)

ROLLY. Okay-okay!

RYKER. Turn it off!

(*Ceasefire*)

CISCO. You surrender?

RYKER. To you?

AMELIA. To us.

ROLLY. Never!

(*Amelia douses Ryker and Rolly again*)

RYKER. Run away!

ROLLY. Run away!

(*Ryker and Rolly flee as Cisco and Amelia celebrate*)

AMELIA. Perfect!

CISCO. Give me a turn.

(Amelia passes the hose to Cisco, standing at the ready.

Ryker and Rolly return)

RYKER. Put the hose down. We call for a cease-fire.

CISCO. Surrender unconditionally.

ROLLY. Never!

(Cisco gives them a warning spray. Ryker kicks Rolly)

RYKER. Shut up and let me do the talking!

AMELIA. What do you want?

ROLLY. The traitor's head on a platter!

(Cisco lets Rolly have it with the hose)

AMELIA. Hang on. Let's hear them out.

RYKER. You can't come to the peace table with a nuke in your hand.

CISCO. It's a deterrent.

(Amelia turns off the faucet)

AMELIA. Surrender?

RYKER. Escalation.

(Amelia turns the faucet back on)

ROLLY. Cowards!

(Cisco blasts Rolly and Ryker yet again)

RYKER. Damn it, knock it off!

(On Cisco's signal, Amelia turns water off)

CISCO. Surrender your paint.

RYKER. Fine. Rolly.

(Rolly hands over spray paint. Amelia throws them in the garbage)

CISCO. Looks like checkmate.

RYKER. Oh, no-no-no. This match is far from over. I propose a new challenge: me and Rolly vs. you and Amelia.

ROLLY. To the death?

RYKER. To the total humiliation.

AMELIA. We'll do it. When?

RYKER. Now.

CISCO. Wait, it's got to be three in the morning.

RYKER. Amelia already accepted. You bail out, we win.

AMELIA. He's not bailing out.

CISCO. No, I was just saying.

ROLLY. This is gonna be historic.

RYKER. When this night is over, one side will boast bragging rights. And the losers ...

ROLLY. —And the losers have to lick the feet of the victors.

AMELIA. ...

CISCO. Gross.

RYKER. Pervert. You just want Cisco to lick you.

ROLLY. Shut up.

AMELIA. That's nasty. But I'm in.

ROLLY. I'm in.

RYKER. In Cisco?

CISCO. ... Yeah.

AMELIA. I've got something for the test.

CISCO. What?

AMELIA. The train trestle.

CISCO. Perfect.

ROLLY. No way. The train trestle?

RYKER. That's not what I had in mind ...

AMELIA. —You refuse our challenge?

RYKER. No, we just gotta talk ...

AMELIA. —Then we jump off the train trestle into the lake.

RYKER. But people do that all the time.

CISCO. Rolly's never jumped in, and you've only jumped once.

ROLLY. It's the middle of the night!

AMELIA. You expect a test of bravery to be easy?

ROLLY. I never jump in 'cause it's suicide! Know how many people have broken their necks?

CISCO. One. But he just landed wrong.

ROLLY. Oh, that makes me feel better. It's, like, eighty feet high!

AMELIA. It's not eighty ...

ROLLY. —It is, I measured!

AMELIA. Liar.

ROLLY. I ain't going in.

AMELIA. Okay. We win.

RYKER. Wait! (*to Rolly*) Don't be such a wuss! It's only about thirty feet.

AMELIA. Oh, it's more than thirty feet.

CISCO. But the lake is deep enough so we're good.

AMELIA. That's the dare. He chickens out, you forfeit.

RYKER. We're not forfeiting. Rolly, find your ball-sack and do it. I'm going.

(*Ryker exits*)

ROLLY. Hell no. Come on, Cisco.

CISCO. It's not my dare, it's hers.

AMELIA. That's the dare. End of story. Talk to him, Cisco. I'll get towels and meet you down there.

(*Amelia climbs up to her window and exits*)

CISCO. It won't be that bad.

ROLLY. You know I'm not cool with the trestle.

CISCO. We're at war, my friend.

ROLLY. I suck at swimming.

CISCO. The lake is not deep.

ROLLY. But deep enough to jump in from the trestle?

CISCO. That's the only deep part.

ROLLY. Very convincing.

CISCO. You really don't want to do it?

ROLLY. I'm gonna have to now.

CISCO. Why?

ROLLY. Ryker will never let me forget it.

CISCO. Remember how long it took him to jump that time? And he hasn't done it since. There's no way he'll go tonight. I see it in his eyes. He's counting on you to chicken out.

ROLLY. Maybe.

CISCO. Listen. I'll swing it so that Ryker is the one that gives in, okay? Just pretend you're gonna jump. Really play it up. He won't expect that.

ROLLY. You promise? I swear to God if you make me jump ...

CISCO. —I won't. Are you scared of heights?

ROLLY. No. Just scared of falling.

CISCO. Trust me.

ROLLY. Don't tell Ryker I agreed to this.

CISCO. Don't worry.

ROLLY. He'll kill me.

CISCO. I won't say anything.

ROLLY. He will literally kill me. He'll put an untraceable poison in my slushee or something ...

CISCO. —Let's go.

(*Cisco and Rolly exit*)

(TRAIN TRESTLE *over the lake.*

RYKER *stands at the edge of the trestle looking down. He occasionally looks away but the edge draws him back.* AMELIA *enters with towels*)

AMELIA. Don't do it!

(*Ryker startles Amelia laughs*)

RYKER. What the hell? I could've fallen!

AMELIA. I'm sorry.

RYKER. You got a serious mean streak.

AMELIA. Look who's talking.

(*Ryker is drawn back to the edge of the train trestle Amelia joins him there*)

RYKER. That's more than thirty feet.

AMELIA. Yup.

RYKER. Where are those guys?

AMELIA. Cisco's still talking Rolly into it. How often you guys come here?

RYKER. When it's hot. The pool gets crowded with little kids and creepy old men that stare at us.

AMELIA. My brothers took me here for the first time on my tenth birthday. Said they would "make me a man."

RYKER. They did a good job.

(*Amelia rolls with this one*)

AMELIA. We brought Cisco here on his tenth birthday too. Took us an hour to talk him into jumping. Then he wouldn't stop.

RYKER. It's like the one thing he's good at.

AMELIA. He's good at lots of stuff.

RYKER. But not everything, is he?

AMELIA. Oh, you are so sleazy.

RYKER. Just playing around.

AMELIA. What did he tell you?

RYKER. About what?

    (*Amelia punches him in the arm*)

Ow!

AMELIA. What did he tell you?

RYKER. Just that you that you kissed and stuff this summer.

AMELIA. That's it?

RYKER. Yeah. Don't get so pissy.

    (*Beat*)

AMELIA. Ryker? Can I ask you a personal question? Please?

RYKER. Sure.

AMELIA. Why are you such an asshole?

RYKER. Cold.

AMELIA. No, I'm being sincere. I want to help you. Cisco's a great guy, and Rolly seems alright. But you treat them like dirt.

RYKER. You don't get us.

AMELIA. Are you an abused child or something?

RYKER. That must be it. Or maybe I was born evil.

AMELIA. I mean, I see you get picked on at school.

RYKER. Psycho-analyzing me now?

AMELIA. But don't take it out on your friends.

RYKER. You know how ridiculous you sound?

AMELIA. I'm just saying.

RYKER. Now let me ask you a question.

AMELIA. Go ahead.

RYKER. Why didn't you go out with me last year?

AMELIA. Are you talking about that boat dance?

RYKER. Yeah.

AMELIA. You gotta get over that.

RYKER. No, I want to know. What's so bad about me?

AMELIA. Like I told you then, I didn't want to spend a Saturday night hanging out with a bunch of middle schoolers.

RYKER. It had nothing to do with me?

AMELIA. Not really. Cisco even talked you up, trying to get me to go with you.

RYKER. He did?

AMELIA. Yeah.

RYKER. He never told me that.

AMELIA. Probably worried it would bruise your ego. Don't know why.

(Ryker laughs)

RYKER. I am proud of my ego.

AMELIA. Are you laughing at yourself?

RYKER. What, you think I don't have a soul or something?

AMELIA. Sometimes, yeah.

(They both laugh now)

RYKER. I have a soul. I take care of my dog. I listen to jazz. I do community service with the Honor Society. I'm even an honest-to-God Boy Scout.

AMELIA. Seriously?

RYKER. "The few. The strong. The Boy Scouts."

AMELIA. Boy Scout Ryker. I never would have guessed.
(Beat)
You should show this side of yourself more often.

RYKER. See? I'm kind of charming. Attractive.

AMELIA. Tolerable.

RYKER. Must be the moonlight.

AMELIA. I guess.

RYKER. I guess.

(*A pause. Ryker tries to kiss Amelia. She dodges it*)

AMELIA. God, Ryker!

RYKER. Come on. Why not?

AMELIA. Just because a girl talks to you don't mean she wants to get with you.

RYKER. I know.

AMELIA. Unbelievable.

(*Amelia laughs*)

RYKER. You gave it up to the entire senior class last year. Why not me?

AMELIA. The entire senior class? That what they're saying now? It was only "half" before.

RYKER. Even if it was a quarter, you would still be a slut.

AMELIA. You are a child.

CISCO. (*offstage*) Hey!

AMELIA. A miserable, little child.

RYKER. (*to Cisco*) We're up here!

AMELIA. There are rumors about you too, you know.

RYKER. What rumors?

AMELIA. "Why is Ryker so possessive of Cisco.?" "How come Ryker's never had a girlfriend?" Hmm.

RYKER. ... Nuh-uh. Nobody's ... no one's saying that.

(CISCO *and* ROLLY *enter*)

CISCO. ... You two alright?

AMELIA. Just chit-chatting.

RYKER. You look pretty pathetic, Rolly. Chickening out?

CISCO. He's jumping.

AMELIA. He is?

ROLLY. Hell yeah.

RYKER. It's more than thirty feet. Look down.

CISCO. Do not look down.

AMELIA. You'll psyche yourself out.

RYKER. I just don't want him to pee his pants when he sees.

CISCO. He'll be fine.

AMELIA. So? Who goes first?

RYKER. You guys do. It's your dare.

AMELIA. Fine by me.

CISCO. Me too.

RYKER. Amelia first. Then Cisco.

AMELIA. I'm already gone ...

CISCO. —No! Pairs jump together. Got it? At the same time.

AMELIA. Uh ... okay.

CISCO. After we go, you guys have to jump. At the same time.

RYKER. That's dangerous. We can't jump at the ... (same time.)

CISCO. —You cool with that, Rolly?

ROLLY. Same time. Yeah.

RYKER. Want us to hold hands too?

ROLLY. Come here, honey-bun.

(Rolly tries to mock hold hands with Ryker)

RYKER. Gay! Get away from me!

AMELIA. Woo, look at that. Defensive.

CISCO. Everyone agree to the rules?

ROLLY. Yup.

RYKER. Just do it.

AMELIA. Meet us down below with the towels. Bring our clothes too, but don't steal them.

CISCO. You steal our clothes, you automatically lose.

ROLLY. I promise.

RYKER. I wouldn't steal your clothes. I'd burn them.

(Cisco strips down to boxers. Amelia strips down to shorts and sports bra)

ROLLY. Check her out.

RYKER. Not bad.

AMELIA. Pigs. What do you think of Cisco, Ryker? He's looking fit, yeah?

RYKER. Keep it up.

CISCO. What?

AMELIA. Inside joke.

CISCO. Call up when you're in position.

RYKER. Call down when you chicken out.

ROLLY. We're outta here.

AMELIA. See you in a bit, boys.

(*Rolly and Ryker exit with clothes and towels. Cisco stands at the edge*)

CISCO. That is more than thirty feet.

AMELIA. Don't look down.

CISCO. Too late. Water looks scarier when it's pitch black.

AMELIA. It's the same water we always jump into.

CISCO. I don't think so. That's demon blood.

AMELIA. You know what I'm thinking?

CISCO. I hope so. Because you're looking fine in that bra.

AMELIA. Pigs, everyone last one of you. But anyway ... I'm thinking we should pull a Heart Attack.

CISCO. Oh, you are bad. You are so bad.

AMELIA. Come on, it'll be fun! But you have to do it.

CISCO. I've never done it.

AMELIA. You'll do fine.

CISCO. Why me?

AMELIA. Just trust me, it'll be great.

CISCO. So, so bad.

(*Beat*)

AMELIA. Guess what. Ryker just tried to kiss me.

CISCO. He did?

AMELIA. That kid is too much. He goes, "Must be the moonlight," and he comes at me with his mouth open.

CISCO. Nasty.

AMELIA. Can you believe it?

CISCO. You let him kiss you?

AMELIA. No!

CISCO. Would you let me?

AMELIA. Let you what?

CISCO. Kiss you.

AMELIA. You're as bad as he is.

CISCO. But I might die when we jump.

AMELIA. Oh, please.

CISCO. Seriously!

(*Beat*)

Seriously. Let me kiss you.

AMELIA. How many times do we have to do this? It's weird kissing you.
We're like brother and sister.

CISCO. We can imagine we're kissing someone else.

AMELIA. Who would you imagine?

CISCO. I don't know. Sappho, maybe.

AMELIA. Who?

CISCO. Greek poetess.

AMELIA. ... Such a dork.

CISCO. I wouldn't have to imagine. I want to kiss you.

AMELIA. Cisco! You make me feel icky when you talk like this.

CISCO. If I kissed you — hypothetically! — who would you imagine?

AMELIA. Ugh.

CISCO. I want to know who I'm up against.

AMELIA. I don't know. Nobody.

CISCO. Come on. Who are you hot for? And don't lie. I'll know.

AMELIA. You wouldn't understand.

CISCO. Amelia. If you kissed me, who would you pretend I am?

ROLLY. (*offstage, from below*) Okay! We're ready for you!

AMELIA. (*calling down*) We're on our way! (*to Cisco*) Let's go.

CISCO. Just a little one.

AMELIA. Want a kiss? Fine.

(*Amelia stands there passively as Cisco kisses her. He's into it. She is not*)

CISCO. Mmm.

AMELIA. Satisfied?

CISCO. Thanks. You feel anything? At all?

AMELIA. You got what you wanted, didn't you?

RYKER. (*offstage, from below*) Come on! Let's go!

CISCO. (*calling down*) Hold on! (*to Amelia*) You ready?

AMELIA. I've been ready. You're the one talking.

(*They stand at the edge*)

CISCO. Still wanna do the Heart Attack?

RYKER. (*off-stage, from below*) You got ten seconds until you lose!

AMELIA. Definitely.

CISCO. Okay. This is gonna be ugly. (*calling down*) Here we go!

ROLLY. (*off-stage, from below*) We're ready!

(*Amelia grabs Cisco's hand*)

AMELIA/CISCO. One! Two! Three!

(*Darkness. They scream*)

(*The shore of* THE LAKE, *below the trestle. A few moments earlier.*
CISCO *and* ROLLY *enter*)

RYKER. They won't do it. Cisco doesn't realize how high it is.

ROLLY. He and Amelia jump all the time.

RYKER. Not at night, they don't.

ROLLY. (*calling up*) Okay! We're ready for you!

AMELIA. (*off-stage, calling down*) We're on our way!

(*Ryker and Rolly stare up, waiting*)

ROLLY. You ever see the crazy stunts Amelia's brothers do? Diving head first, flips, pushing each other off. They've got to have a death wish.

RYKER. I hope Amelia does too.

ROLLY. Don't say that. Not even joking.

RYKER. (*calling up*) Come on! Let's go!

CISCO. (*off-stage, calling down*) Hold on!

ROLLY. There're gonna do it. I'm gonna be sick. Please God, don't kill them.

RYKER. Just maim Amelia.

ROLLY. Don't even joke like that!

(*Beat*)

RYKER. Rolly? You hear people saying stuff about me? At school?

ROLLY. They say you're a little prick.

RYKER. (*calling up*) You got ten seconds 'til you lose!
(*to Rolly*)
I know that. But ... anything else?

ROLLY. Like what?

CISCO. (*calling down*) Here we go!

ROLLY. (*off-stage, from below*) We're ready!

AMELIA/CISCO. (*off-stage, from above*) One! Two! Three!

> (*They scream offstage. Rolly screams too.*
> *Rolly and Ryker watch them fall off-stage*)

ROLLY. Ah! Oh, my God!

> (*A splash as they hit the water off-stage*)

RYKER. You see them?

> (*They look*)

ROLLY. No!

RYKER. Should ... should we go in?

> (*They look*)

ROLLY. Go in!

RYKER. Come with me!

ROLLY. I can't swim!

        (*Amelia screams off-stage*)

ROLLY. Oh-my-God. Oh-my-God!

AMELIA. (*off-stage*) Get in here! Quick!

ROLLY. Go, Ryker

AMELIA. (*off-stage*) It's Cisco!

RYKER. Shit!

        (*Ryker runs off to help Amelia. Rolly reacts to what he sees and hears happening off-stage*)

AMELIA. (*off-stage*) Get him to shore!

RYKER. (*off-stage*) Don't move his neck!

ROLLY. No! No!

RYKER. (*off-stage*) Go call an ambulance!

AMELIA. (*off-stage*) No, help us get him out first!

> (*Rolly runs off to help.* AMELIA, RYKER, *and* ROLLY *return carefully holding an unconscious* CISCO)

ROLLY. Is he breathing?

AMELIA. You know CPR?

RYKER. Get him on firm ground.

> (*They lay Cisco down*)

AMELIA. Hurry!

RYKER. Let me think! Uh ... Okay. I can do this.
> (*He checks Cisco's pulse*)

Heart's going crazy. But I think that's good.

ROLLY. He's not breathing!

AMELIA. Mouth to mouth!

RYKER. Okay!

(Ryker begins mouth to mouth resuscitation. Cisco shoves him away)

CISCO. Gay! Try to kiss me?

(Amelia bursts out laughing)

ROLLY. What?!

RYKER. Not cool. Not cool!

ROLLY. You gave me a heart attack!

AMELIA. That's why they call it a Heart Attack.

CISCO. Amelia's brother did that to me once.

ROLLY. That was sick. Not funny at all.

AMELIA. And Ryker was the sweetest little Boy Scout, saving his friend's life.

RYKER. Shut up.

AMELIA. And kissing him too.

RYKER. Shut up!

CISCO. At least he got one kiss tonight.

AMELIA. "Must be the moonlight."

(*They laugh. The coldest glare from Ryker*)

ROLLY. I don't get it.

AMELIA. Inside joke.

CISCO. Give me a towel.

(*Cisco and Amelia dry off and dress*)

AMELIA. Alright, guys. Your turn.

(*Rolly turns desperately to Cisco. He winks reassurance*)

CISCO. Head on up.

RYKER. I'm not going. Not after that stunt you pulled.

ROLLY. Uhh. How's the water?

CISCO. Refreshing.

AMELIA. You'll love it. It feels warmer at night.

CISCO. It does, doesn't it? But it's terrifying underwater. I opened my eyes.

AMELIA. Me too!

CISCO. Could you see anything?

AMELIA. Pitch black.

RYKER. Bravo. Bra-vo.

CISCO. Go on. Trestle's waiting.

RYKER. No. I'm pissed.

ROLLY. Let's rock.

(*Rolly strips down to his underwear briefs*)

RYKER. Oh. God.

CISCO. Rolly you should really wear boxers.

ROLLY. Mom buys tighty-whities. Wholesale. Says they're more snug and safe.

AMELIA. Please stop talking.

ROLLY. Come on, Ryker. Our turn.

RYKER. What happened to the trestle being suicide?

ROLLY. Found my ball-sack.

    (*Rolly grabs himself for emphasis. Cisco and Amelia both laugh*)

AMELIA. Strip, Ryker.

RYKER. Hold on.

    (*Ryker sizes up the trestle, then water*)

CISCO. Don't think about it. You'll lose your nerve.

AMELIA. Maybe he won't take his clothes off because he's hiding something.

ROLLY. (*to Ryker*) Got wood?

RYKER. Get away from me.

AMELIA. Kissing Cisco must have been exhilarating.

CISCO. I'm flattered.

RYKER. Suck it, you guys. Go ahead, Rolly. I'm right behind you.

ROLLY. Nuh-uh. If I have to take my clothes off, so do you.

CISCO. Yeah. That's part of the dare too.

RYKER. You can't do that! You never said ...

AMELIA. —We just did.

RYKER. You change rules like that, that's cheating. I'm not doing it.

ROLLY. It's cool. If you're not comfortable doing it, we won't do it.

RYKER. You'd like that, wouldn't you? Blame all this on me?

ROLLY. Look at me. I'm ready to go.

AMELIA. Oh, and one more thing.

RYKER. No more rule changes!

AMELIA. You guys do have to hold hands when you jump.

CISCO. Awesome.

ROLLY. I'm cool with that. Ryker?

RYKER. Hell. No.

CISCO. We did.

RYKER. I'm not holding hands! It's gay enough you guys want us to get all naked together.

CISCO. Then you fail on the final dare.

ROLLY. They've got us, Ryker..

RYKER. ...

CISCO. Oh, he's pissed.

AMELIA. But he's not saying anything, so ... we win!

(*Cisco and Amelia do obnoxious victory dance*)

RYKER. Hold on, hold on. It's not over.

CISCO. You lost, sucka!

AMELIA. What do the losers have to do again?

(*Cisco points to his feet*)

Oh, yeah! Lick our feet. You know I've got athlete's foot, don't you?

RYKER. I'm not done yet!

ROLLY. They won, fair and square.

(*Rolly gets dressed*)

RYKER. Fair and square, my ass. I started this, I end it. They change the rules, so do I.

CISCO. You're such a sore loser.

AMELIA. He's a loser period.

RYKER. I'd rather be a loser than a big dyke.

(*Beat*)

AMELIA. ... What did you just call me?

RYKER. A dyke. Means lesbian. Means a girl who wants to have sex with other girls. Are you a dyke?

AMELIA. ...

RYKER. Oh. Oh! Wow. This is a new land of opportunity. A lesbian America.

AMELIA. You shut your mouth right now.

CISCO. Come on, let's just ...

RYKER. —Everything makes sense now. Why you slept around with so many senior guys last year ...

AMELIA. —Shut up!

RYKER. No one suspects you're a dyke when you're a slut, right?

CISCO. Ryker!

RYKER. But when Cisco. wanted some, you couldn't go through with it. You cried because "it just didn't feel right." Isn't that what you told me, Cisco?

AMELIA. (*to Cisco*) ... You lying sack of shit.

RYKER. Broke his heart. But you're just not into him "that way."

(*Amelia tackles Ryker and starts pounding on him. Ryker tries to laugh through his pain*)

ROLLY. Fight!

CISCO. Amelia!

RYKER. (*to Amelia*) Look at you!

AMELIA. These guys don't have the balls to give you an ass-kicking.

RYKER. But you have the balls, don't you?

(*Amelia pounds again until Cisco tries to pull her off. She is stronger*)

CISCO. Don't let him get to you!

(*Amelia stops*)

RYKER. Get off me.

(*Cisco helps Amelia up while Rolly starts to help Ryker up*)

ROLLY. Don't mess with her. You'll lose.

RYKER. Thanks for backing me up, stupid Roland.

(*Hearing this, Rolly drops Ryker back on the ground,
his foot on Ryker's chest*)

ROLLY. You will never call me that again. Got it?

RYKER. ...

CISCO. Yeah, Rolly.

ROLLY. If you do, I will beat you down quicker and worser than she just did.

AMELIA. I didn't lay into him half as much as I could have.

ROLLY. Got it?

(*Ryker tries shoving Rolly's foot off, but he's pinned to the ground*)

RYKER. Just get off of ...

(*Another unsuccessful attempt*)

—Who cares what I call you?

ROLLY. Never again.

CISCO. Do what he says.

RYKER. Okay.

ROLLY. Okay what?

AMELIA. He's really milking this.

CISCO. Say it.

RYKER. I'll never call you "stupid Roland" again.

ROLLY. And apologize to Amelia..

RYKER. I'm not gonna ... [apologize]

ROLLY. —Apologize!

(*Beat*)

RYKER. I'm sorry.

(*Beat*)

AMELIA. Let him up.

(*Rolly lets Ryker up*)

RYKER. (*to Rolly*) You're a bigger asshole than these guys.

(*to Amelia*)

Yeah, I'm sorry, Amelia. I should be celebrating the fact that you're a lesbian.

ROLLY. You're out of control.

RYKER. Where's your tolerance? We need to accept our gay friends.

    (*Beat*)

Unless ... you're uncomfortable because ... you are also ...

ROLLY. —Me? What?

RYKER. I know. I know, I was just messing with you.

    (*indicates Cisco and Amelia*)

But these two ...

AMELIA. Ryker?

RYKER. Yes, Lezlie?

AMELIA. You are a soulless turd.

RYKER. I hurt your feelings? I thought lesbians were tough.

AMELIA. —Stop saying that.

RYKER. Well, you did just kick my ass, so ...

AMELIA. —For the record ...

CISCO. —No, Amelia. He's trapping you ...

AMELIA. —You shut up!

RYKER. Very manly.

AMELIA. I am not a lesbian. No more rumors.

CISCO. Leave it alone.

AMELIA. I can prove it.

RYKER. Prove it?

ROLLY. Whoa.

CISCO. You don't have to prove anything.

AMELIA. I'll prove it to all three of you.

RYKER. Right now?

ROLLY. Whoa ...

CISCO. —No!

ROLLY. Whoa! This is it!

RYKER. Make men out of us?

AMELIA. I'll do anything you want. But you have to go first, Ryker.
Take your clothes off.

RYKER. Why me?

AMELIA. Because you got something to prove too. Don't you?

> (*Amelia drops to her knees*)

CISCO. Stop! Stop it!

> (*Cisco picks Amelia up on her feet*)

AMELIA. Let go of me!

CISCO. —You're not thinking straight.

RYKER. Never has, never will.

CISCO. You're the biggest asshole of all time, Ryker. But you win.

AMELIA. I'm not licking anyone's feet.

CISCO. But you'll do everything else?

    (*to Ryker*)

Want me to lick your feet? I'll do it. But this ends now.

RYKER. Tempting to see you bow down before me.

CISCO. Amelia doesn't have to. Just me. And you don't say anything about her at school. You don't even look at her.

AMELIA. ...

RYKER. What do you think, Rolly?

ROLLY. I don't mind if Amelia does the first thing, you know?

CISCO. I hate you, Rolly.

ROLLY. Me? What did I do?

CISCO. I hate you too, Ryker. But what do you want me to do?

RYKER. Fine. Lick our feet, then the game is over. Rolly.'s first.

ROLLY. Why me?

RYKER. Take off your shoes.

(*Rolly takes off his shoes*)

CISCO. Amelia.'s safe, right?

RYKER. We won't say a word.

CISCO. You promise?

RYKER. Scout's honor.

AMELIA. Cisco, don't.

CISCO. Leave!

(*Amelia leaves*)

RYKER. Lick.

CISCO. We're done.

(*Cisco licks Rolly's foot*)

ROLLY. Gross.

CISCO. Satisfied?

RYKER. Yeah. I see you liked it.

    (*to Rolly*)

Why did you let him do that?

ROLLY. You gotta do it too. Take your shoes off.

RYKER. I'm not letting a guy lick my feet, stupid Roland.

ROLLY. What did I just tell ... ?

RYKER —Quiet

ROLLY. ...

CISCO. We're done.

RYKER. We were done the moment you betrayed me.

CISCO. You're pathetic. Both of you are.

RYKER. Maybe. But you are alone now. Checkmate.

(*Ryker exits*)

ROLLY. Things got out of hand.

CISCO. Get away from me.

ROLLY. I'm the one that should be pissed. I was about lose some kind of virginity tonight.

CISCO. You make me sick.

ROLLY. Jeez. Be a bitch about it.

CISCO. Yeah, that's me. A gay wuss pussy bitch. Anything else? Slap it on me. I'll wear it with pride.

ROLLY. I'll call you when this blows over.

CISCO. I won't answer. We're done.

ROLLY. I said I was sorry!

CISCO. But I don't forgive you.

ROLLY. I don't get you, man. I'm the only friend you got now.

(*Rolly exits.*

A few moments later, AMELIA *enters*)

AMELIA. Hey.

CISCO. Don't say anything.

AMELIA. Don't worry. You'll get new friends. That's how it is.

CISCO. You don't know.

AMELIA. I do know. And it's not much, but you got me.

CISCO. You're so stupid.

AMELIA. Stupid?

CISCO. Because you don't realize how amazing you are.

AMELIA. Cisco.

CISCO. I don't know where you went tonight. I lost you. Like you disappeared in the water.

AMELIA. But I came back.

CISCO. You still mean everything to me, even if I think ... even if I know that nothing is gonna come of it.

AMELIA. ... You'll find someone.

CISCO. I don't want to.

AMELIA. But you will.

CISCO. I can't look at you right now. Okay? Please. Just go home.

AMELIA. Okay.

> (*She stays.*
>
> *They wait.*
>
> *Dawn*)

CISCO. Look. The sun's coming up.

END OF PLAY

www.ingramcontent.com/pod-product-compliance
Lightning Source LLC
Chambersburg PA
CBHW080753120626
46557CB00005B/1244